D0571689

Interplanetary Avenger

Interplanetary Avenger

CAROLINE LUZZATTO

HOLIDAY HOUSE / New York

Library of Congress Cataloging-in-Publication Data

Luzzatto, Caroline.
Interplanetary avenger / Caroline Luzzatto.— 1st ed.
p. cm.
Summary: When Sam accidentally opens a strange box and finds himself
sitting in the principal's office of an intergalactic middle school, he is pressed
to take on the challenge of capturing an obnoxious shape-shifting alien.
ISBN 0-8234-1933-9
[1. Extraterrestrial beings—Fiction. 2. Schools—Fiction.
3. Humorous stories.] I. Title.

PZ7.L9795545In 2005
[Fic]—dc22   2004058834

ISBN-13: 978-0-8234-1933-3
ISBN-10: 0-8234-1933-9

To Henry, Michael, Katharine, and especially Donald, who all deserve extra-large helpings of love, gratitude, and squash casserole.

Interplanetary Avenger

Chapter One

Maybe I should be used to finding myself in strange places by now. It certainly isn't anything new.

We move a lot, and it always seems to be in the middle of the school year. I never know anybody, which gets to be a drag.

Usually when I start off at a new school, something happens during the first few days that gives me an idea of how things are going to go. At one school I stepped up to the plate and hit a home run during my first baseball game with my new gym class. When the ball hit the ground, it took off on a bouncing roll and ended up stuck under a "portable classroom," which was what the school called the trailers they set up when they started running out of room in the main building. It was a fluke—I have never been very good at baseball. But it didn't matter—everybody thought it was pretty cool that I made the gym teacher shout and spend half of class fishing the ball out with the janitor's push broom. I never wanted to leave that school, but we only lasted there for a year.

Most of the time, however, it turns out the way it did here—Furniss J. Hotchkiss Middle School. After a couple of days wandering through my classes and not knowing anyone, I was facing another lunch alone in the cafeteria. I stood in line, waiting for food, not talking to anyone. I really was minding my own business.

Apparently I am one of those people that fate just doesn't like.

"Hey," said a voice behind me. "Hey! You got my fruit cocktail."

I turned around. A large, unpleasant face leaned close to mine. "That was the last fruit cocktail. That was mine."

I looked at the buffet. It was true—the fruit cocktail had been replaced by butterscotch pudding.

"There's pudding," I said, turning away and pushing my tray.

"I don't like pudding," the guy said.

"Yeah? Neither do I," I said over my shoulder.

Exactly how long is this conversation going to go on? I wondered. We sounded like old men arguing about the dessert menu at our retirement village.

I paid for my lunch and sat down at the empty end of a table. Some guys at the other end were discussing skateboard moves. I started eating.

Then across from me appeared the fruit-cocktail guy. He sat down, flanked by two of his friends. They were all large. Perhaps it was all the fruit cocktail they ate.

"You forgot to give me my fruit cocktail," the guy said.

I groaned. Who *was* this guy?

"Fine," I said. "Take it." Lunch really wasn't going my way. I got up, planning to go sit somewhere else.

Mr. Fruit Cocktail and his friends were laughing. I walked around the table. And that's when it happened. A couple of kids pushed past me on one side, and another tried to squeeze past me going the other way. They were all carrying trays, and one of them tripped over my foot. The tray slid out of the kid's hand, and instead of just letting it fall, I tried to catch it. But I didn't get a very good grip. As the tray tilted, all the food on it slid to one side, and then spilled over . . . onto the back of the fruit-cocktail guy. He managed a startled, "Huh?" and then just froze, furious, as pizza slid along his back, corn and peas scattered over his shoulders, and cold butterscotch pudding dripped down his collar.

"Oops," I said.

Actually "oops" does not even begin to cover it. Mr. Fruit Cocktail, whose name is Bradley, seemed to be a little upset with me. The next day in gym, he threw a basketball directly at my face. "Heads up!" he yelled cheerfully, after the ball had already bounced off my nose.

The day after that, he got behind me in the hallway and stepped on the back of my shoe over and over, until it flipped off entirely. Then he helpfully picked it up and threw it into a trash can. Not only did I have to dive in after it, but the whole thing made me late for computer class. I ended up with the computer that had a broken mouse and brown goo on the keyboard that everybody said marked the spot where some kid threw up.

But it didn't really get bad until the golden retriever showed up.

Actually it was one of those cheesy bumper stickers that says, "I ❤ my golden retriever," with a picture of a dog's head on it. While standing at my locker, I felt a heavy thwack on my back. It was Bradley, slapping the sticker onto me.

As pranks go it was a pointless one, even by Bradley's standards. Where's the humor? I wondered as I peeled the sticker off my shirt.

"What's wrong?" Bradley asked. "Don't you like your cute sticker?"

I was turning to walk away from him, holding the sticker in my hands, when he stuck out his foot. I tried to step over it but stepped on one of his friends' feet instead, stumbled forward, and fell against the lockers on the other side of the hallway. The sticker smacked against one of the lockers and stuck.

I heard scattered laughter—then an ominous silence.

"Young man!" said a familiar voice. The gym teacher was looming over me. "Vandalism is *not* permitted in this school."

Bradley walked up behind the coach. "I saw him do it!"

"To the office!" the gym teacher said, glaring at me.

"But—" I sputtered.

"I'll escort you there myself," he said. As we walked down the hall, I looked back to see Bradley and his friends laughing like hyenas.

So there I was, sitting in the row of chairs lined up along the wall, waiting for a talk with the principal. Another kid sat in one of the chairs, holding his backpack and lunch box, looking miserable. The secretary was answering the constantly ringing phone. On one wall was a poster with a kitten hanging by its claws from a tree branch. It said, HANG IN THERE. FRIDAY IS COMING. On the chair next to me was an old, sticky juice box with a smiling-bunch-of-grapes picture on it.

The secretary hadn't even said anything to me because she was still on the phone. The principal's door opened as a teacher walked out, and the secretary just pointed at me with a pencil, then pointed at the doorway.

I walked into the principal's office and sat down on a hard wooden chair. "So, you felt the need to add a decoration to our school?" asked a pile of notebooks.

Then the principal stood up, and I realized that

it had only looked like the notebooks were speaking to me. His desk was so heaped with books and papers that there could have been a couple more people back there, and I never would have known.

"It was an accident," I said.

"Vandalism is not an accident," he said.

"But I didn't mean to put up the sticker. I just fell—"

"Young man, there are no excuses in this office."

"Yes sir," I said. It was actually kind of hard to concentrate on the principal. A stack of papers on his desk was leaning to the left, on the verge of falling over. I watched it, waiting for the avalanche.

"What does that poster say?" He pointed to a framed picture on the wall of people holding hands.

"'Together we can do it.'"

"That's right. Together we can make this school work."

I nodded.

"Now this is a busy time for all of us. We're in the middle of testing, and it's important that we all do our part. What bothers me about vandalism is that it's so pointless. We can't waste time and energy on foolish behavior."

"But sir—"

He slapped a hand down on top of the slowly collapsing paper pile to keep it steady. "Yes?"

"I don't even *have* a golden retriever," I said.

The principal sat back down behind his mountainous desk with a sigh. "Detention," said the pile of notebooks.

And that was that. I spent two days cleaning graffiti off desks and the rest of the week trying to avoid Bradley. Neither of these activities worked very well. There still seemed to be plenty of gunk on everyone's desks, and Bradley made it his mission in life to make me miserable, at least until some other target came along.

I walked home from school today with a bloody nose and a couple of pages ripped out of my math book. The way things have been going lately, that doesn't even count as a very bad day, just an average one.

Chapter Two

When I got home, sitting there in the middle of the driveway was a box—an ordinary-looking box, only without an address label or a name; nothing but a sticker with black lettering in all sorts of odd languages I couldn't remember ever seeing before. There was one part I could understand, though. Near the top in big, black letters, it said DO NOT OPEN.

It said, "Do not open," not "Do not touch," so I figured there wouldn't be much harm in at least checking it out. After all, what could really go wrong? But when I tried to lift the box, it wouldn't budge. Too heavy.

And there was something else strange about it. Although it looked like it was just a cardboard box, it felt odd—it was cool and hard like metal and seemed to be vibrating just the tiniest bit. I put my ear against it and heard a buzz inside like an angry fly.

"Do not open," I said, rubbing my chin. "But how would you open it, anyway?" The box was smooth and seamless and didn't seem to have any place where it could be opened. I rubbed my hands over the top, then the sides, and was about to give up when I felt something—a tiny loop of string, about as thick as dental floss. I hooked my finger in it and gave it a little tug.

There was a pop, and the loop of string ripped off the package.

"Great," I said. It must have just come off without opening anything. All I had now was a little piece of string looped around my finger.

"Well, forget it," I said to myself, and turned to go inside to get something to eat.

As I turned around something caught the corner of my eye—a little glimmer of light. The package was shimmering. For a moment it looked as if it was made of glowing, fluorescent TV static, then it looked like a sort of glittering mist. A little tendril of that mist snaked around my ankle, then another reached around my wrist, then another seemed to flow right into my ear, which really tickled.

In an instant I was surrounded by the mist. Before I could even open my mouth to call for help, a face appeared in front of me.

My face.

I reached out and touched it. It was real.

It was wearing my exact shoes and one of them was untied, just like mine.

There was my shirt, with a blotch of toothpaste on the collar. I pulled my own shirt down a bit so I could see the collar. Exactly the same, right down to the blotch.

I poked it in the stomach with my finger.

It poked me back.

I nudged its foot with my foot.

It nudged me back.

I waved hello.

It licked its pinky and stuck its wet finger in my ear. I shuddered and pulled away. I hate wet willies.

"Hey . . . ," I croaked. The exact copy of me grinned back at me.

"Sucker!" the other me said. He cackled. Then he shoved me backward. The mist held me up for just a second before it all seemed to dissolve, and I fell flat on my back.

And I had no more than stood back up when the

next extremely weird thing happened. There was a bright flash of light, I felt a sickening lurch in my stomach as if I was riding on the world's fastest elevator, and then—*Pop!*—I suddenly found myself staring into a slimy, angry, not-at-all human face.

Chapter Three

A dark green, squid-shaped secretary adjusted her glasses with a damp-looking tentacle and said, "Argle doop."

I stood and stared.

I was standing in a place that looked like the waiting room outside the school principal's office—a squid-secretary sitting in front of a computer, phones ringing, and a couple of unhappy-looking guys sitting in a row of chairs, waiting for their appointments with doom.

Except these people weren't like anyone at my school. In fact, as far as I could tell, these people weren't people at all.

The squid-secretary gave an impatient sort of huff. "Ip giddle bo!" She pointed to the row of chairs with one tentacle, while sorting through a file folder with two others.

I stared, open-mouthed. Out the window I could see pink clouds and two suns. It was a very sunny day.

The squid-secretary heaved another sigh and fished something out of her desk with a free tentacle. Then with that same tentacle, she slapped me behind the ear. It felt like getting whacked with a plate of cold Jell-O.

"How about now?" she said. "*Now* do you understand?"

I nodded. Sure. Right. I understood perfectly. The talking squid had whacked me in the head and now everything made sense.

"*You need to sit in the chair,*" she said loudly and slowly, as if she were talking to a confused kindergartner. "The director will see you shortly."

I began backing over to a chair.

On the wall nearest me was a poster of something that looked like a kitten hanging from a tree branch by its claws. Except the kitten had two heads.

The chair next to me had a juice box sitting on it. I poked the box with my finger. The picture on the front showed something like a smiling, purple pineapple. The writing looked like nothing I'd ever seen before. There was a thin, spider-webby tendril of green slime hanging from the end of the straw.

I decided not to touch anything else.

The squid-secretary pushed a button on her desk and spoke into something that looked a bit like an intercom. "Sir? Can you clear your schedule? We may have a problem." She looked up at me. "Sir, I'm afraid we have a human here."

She leaned closer to the speaker, and her voice dropped to a whisper. "It doesn't seem to be very smart. And it's even uglier in person, sir."

The guy two chairs away leaned over, rolled three of his six eyes, and whispered, "Man, you're in trouble now. What did you do, anyway?"

Chapter Four

I scratched the spot behind my ear where the squid-secretary had whacked me. It felt like a mosquito bite, but stickier.

"The translator node always itches at first," said the six-eyed guy. He was a pale shade of green with a wide, froggy mouth that seemed to stretch all the way from one ear to the other. "It'll get better in a few minutes."

"What?"

He grinned. "The translator. That's why you can understand me."

I nodded.

"You know, once my older brother tinkered with the software somehow so every time someone said,

'Take your seat,' in Thalusian, it sounded to me like, 'Twenty jumping jacks, on the double.' I got detention twice."

"Bummer," I said.

"Yeah, he *never* gets in trouble."

As it turned out the unlucky soul sitting near me was named Mixto, and he had been sent to the director's office for his latest brother-related misfortune. "My brother gave me these stinking fog capsules, but I wasn't going to use them—I just stuck them into my pocket so I could show them to my friends. But I slipped on some Rigelian squash casserole in the cafeteria, and when I fell I must have landed on a couple of capsules." He rolled all six of his eyes. "It's not like the cafeteria smelled that good to begin with."

"I'm sure it didn't, if it's anything like mine," I said. "We had stuffed cabbage the other day, and it smelled like something had died. I don't think they actually cooked it. I think they just left it sitting in the sun for a few days to ferment."

Mixto looked thoughtful. "Actually I think they *do* ferment our squash casserole."

"Maybe it wouldn't be such a bad idea to bring your own lunch," I said.

Mixto laughed. "You're pretty funny for a human."

"Thanks," I said. "I think." Mixto grinned from ear to ear. Literally. "Hey," I said. "Can I ask you something?"

He nodded.

"I was wondering, how did you know I'm from Earth?"

"TV," he said.

"You watch TV?"

"There's this travel show called 'Universal Friendly Observers,' and they do programs about all these places that are still too primitive for regular tourists. Like Earth. And we watch some of your shows, too."

"Our shows?"

"You know, those broadcasts don't just stop at Earth. They radiate into space. And they're some of the most popular shows on the Intergalactic Variety Channel."

"Really? Like which ones?"

"Oh, you know, the classics. 'The Price Is Right,' 'Sabado Gigante,' Oprah, gangster movies, 'Iron Chef,' Barney. Some species don't even need the translators—they watch so much TV that they pick up most of your languages."

I was having a little trouble processing all this. *"Barney?"* I said, feeling weak.

"How's this?" Mixto said, then started singing the Barney song in a deep, croaking voice.

I rested my head in my hands. This was not happening.

He sang louder.

The squid-secretary glided from behind her desk and stopped directly in front of us. "Ahem," she said, fixing Mixto with a nasty glare. He shut up.

She turned to me. "Human," she said. I nodded.

"The director will see you now. Walk this way," she said, pointing a tentacle toward his office as she returned to her desk. "Now what exactly should I put into your file? You're a human . . . what?"

I wasn't sure what she meant. "Ummm . . . a boy, ma'am?" I guessed.

"Right," she said. "Human a Boy." She said it again to herself slowly, as she typed on her keyboard, then looked back up at me. "Well, go on. He hasn't got all day."

I stepped far enough down the hallway to be out

of her view, then stopped to collect my wits. What was left of them, anyway.

From what Mixto had said, this appeared to be a giant alien school—with a cafeteria as extraordinarily bad as my own. But whatever all these creatures thought they knew about humans, I didn't have a clue about them. At least they hadn't come up yet in science class. Normally my response would be to stay quiet and maybe fudge the truth, just a little. But for all I knew, there was some sort of disintegrating lie-detector death beam installed in the director's office. So I decided to fall back on the ol' reliable: Play dumb.

This time it wouldn't be an act.

Chapter Five

"Park your biscuit," said the director.

"Pardon me?" I asked. Even sitting down the director was tall. He leaned forward over a desk piled with mountains of books and papers, and stared at me from behind glasses that seemed to make his eyes swim. Aside from his massive size—this guy must have been seven feet tall—he looked more or less human.

"Your can. Your keister. Park it in the chair."

He flipped through a stack of what looked like fill-in-the-bubble test sheets impatiently, then plunked them down. "You got plucked."

"I'm afraid I don't understand, sir," I said.

He rolled his eyes. It wasn't just his glasses that made them look strange. They swirled like pinwheels.

Just watching them made me feel weak. They were like a cartoon hypnotist's trick. They made me want to do anything he said.

"You were hustled. Picked clean."

I stared at him, dizzy.

"You do speak English, don't you?" he asked. I nodded. My eyes wandered over to the wall, where there was what looked like an old gangster-movie poster, except that one of the bad guys had three arms and the cop in the background was purple. "You were a chump."

"Oh," I said. Now I understood. "If I could just ask—"

He cut me off. "You've just had an unusual experience. I understand why you might be playing with the squirrels."

I wasn't sure what this meant, but I decided to let it go. The director was talking slowly and calmly, as if he was trying to explain something very complicated to someone very simple, and I didn't want to upset him any more. A vein above his eye had already started to throb.

"Is that why I'm here? Is this about the package? Because you can have it back—"

"Silence!" he shouted. "I have no patience for this jibber jabber! Do you have any idea how much trouble you're in? You can read, can't you? Earth schools are pitifully behind the rest of the galaxy, but you have gotten that far, haven't you?"

I nodded.

"And you are aware of what the phrase 'do not open' means, are you not?"

I nodded.

"And yet you proceeded to open a certain . . . package, correct?"

I nodded. The director's voice was growing louder with each question.

"Even though that meant putting *all living things in eighty-five surrounding solar systems in great danger and causing a great deal of inconvenience to the Central Denebian Accelerated School for Expatriate Space Travelers and Associated Mutants?*" By the time he finished, he was standing up, waving his arms, and shouting. A wave of his gasoline-scented breath washed over me. A few flecks of spit popped out of his mouth and fell, sizzling, onto the desk.

I held onto my chair with both hands and froze, waiting for him to leap over the desk and bite off my head. As I stared up at him, I realized I had been wrong about his height. He was at least seven feet six, maybe even eight feet tall.

He took a deep breath, straightened his tie, and sat back down.

"Very well," he said. "That package was my responsibility. Inside was a certain individual, serving interplanetary detention. The package was . . . misdirected, shall we say, and it ended up in your driveway, it appears. Which would have been fine. But before we could retrieve it, you opened it. When we initiated the transport field, all we picked up was *you*."

"I'm sorry, sir," I said. "It was kind of an accident."

"Well, the contents of that package are, as we speak, wreaking all kinds of havoc, and we're not permitted to go down there to straighten things out. Your primitive planet remains under quarantine. Travel to and from it is severely restricted. I shudder to think what Exeter Lar Junderpanz is capable of doing down there."

The director rubbed his chin. "Which brings us to you. What do you think we should do about you?"

I tried to look innocent, but his whirling eyes were making me wobble in my chair.

24

"All right, I'll give you a choice. You can go back to try to repair the damage you did, or . . ." He raised an eyebrow.

"Or?" I asked.

"Well, I suppose we could send you to detention for a few years. Long enough to write, 'Even primitive humans know better than to open boxes that don't belong to them' eighty-four quintillion times."

"Maybe I could go back, sir."

"I knew you'd make the right choice," he said with a smile that I didn't entirely believe. I must have appeared a little doubtful because he looked me up and down for a long moment, then added, "Do not be alarmed, Human. I'm sure you won't end up . . . sleeping with the fishes."

Chapter Six

"I'm Axolotl, and I'll be your instructor today," said an alarmingly lizardlike creature, pacing back and forth in the small room. He had a whistle hanging from a string around his neck and a hat with a hologram of a sort of slug with a mohawk on it. He was wearing really ugly polyester shorts.

The director had sent me down the hall for what he called "a briefing," before I was to be sent back to Earth to do whatever it was I was supposed to do. I was still not quite clear on the whole idea, but the director had called it "a learning experience" and "an opportunity to show initiative." Then he seemed to get distracted after a flurry of questions over the intercom from the squid-secretary about some kind of inspection.

"What should I call you?" Axolotl asked.

"Umm, Sam is fine," I said.

"All right, Sam," he said. "You are here." He drew an X on a sort of blackboard suspended in midair. "We're going to send you back here." He drew a dotted line, then a circle. "The package was supposed to go here." He drew another X. "Apparently there were some gravitational problems during delivery." He drew a series of wiggly lines.

And he went on like that for another minute or two, checking his watch the whole time, until the board looked like a page out of a demented football playbook.

"Understand?" he asked.

"No," I said.

"Good," he said. "Now here's your interplanetary transport device. Just tap the button to transport yourself back here when you're done. Understand?"

"Not really," I said.

"Okay, now you'll be rounding up . . ." He flipped through a little notebook. "Aha! Exeter. Well, that should be a challenge."

"But how—"

"Remember," Axolotl said. "Buterian mutants

are shape-shifters. They can alter the size and shape of other creatures, too, if they get close enough. They also have quite a bit of mechanical aptitude. Always do well in shop class." His attention seemed to drift away for a moment as he pondered this.

"Anyway, you'll be fine, as long as you don't let him touch you. In any case, I've heard"—his voice dropped to a whisper—"they're really just a bunch of crybabies. Don't let him fool ya."

"But I have to be at school—"

Axolotl tapped his foot impatiently. The bottoms of his feet had a funny sort of grid on them, as if he had built-in tennis shoes. "We all have things to do. We're in the middle of an inspection by the Intergalactic School Accrediting Team, and you don't hear all of us complaining."

"I really don't have time," I said, desperately hoping for some way out.

"Take your time," he said. His voice dropped to a whisper. "Just between us, it would be fine if Exeter stayed gone until the inspection is over."

"But I—"

"Okay! Time's up! I have a test to give." He blew his whistle. "Up! On your feet! Hustle! Hustle!" He pulled me to my feet and started jogging me out the door. "Go team!"

Then he reached down, tapped the button on my transport device, and stepped back, giving his whistle one more toot.

There was a flash of light, a stomach-churning lurch, and all of a sudden, I was back in my driveway.

The sun was shining, the birds were singing, and everything looked perfectly normal.

I just needed to find a crazy escaped alien, capture him somehow, and return him to his jailers without getting melted or disintegrated or whatever bad things happened to people who zip through outer space on a regular basis.

Then again I also had to do my math homework with a grubby, mangled book missing a chunk of Chapter Four.

I guess life is only capable of changing so much at once.

Chapter Seven

I woke up the next morning, feeling much better. Outside, birds were chirping. The sun was just coming up. It was a beautiful day.

I had spent all evening with a baseball bat and a flashlight hidden under my covers, waiting for Exeter to appear. Nothing. The only strange alien sight I saw all night was my scabby brother, Harold, admiring himself in the bathroom mirror for an eternity while I was trying to get in. Except for the fact that I had that transporter jammed in my pocket, I was starting to wonder if it had all been some sort of hallucination. Everything just felt so—normal.

And then I walked to the bathroom.

The light was on, and the door was ajar. There was a strange slurping noise coming from inside.

I peeked in and saw something that would have frightened those happy chirping birds right out of the trees.

Exeter—still looking exactly like me—was dipping Harold's toothbrush into the toilet, then slurping the toilet water off it. He gave a deep sigh of pleasure. Then he started going through the medicine cabinet. He pulled out a tube of Harold's zit cream, squeezed some of it onto Harold's toothbrush, and started brushing his teeth. As he brushed Exeter made little *mmmm-mmmm* sounds as if he were really enjoying the taste. Then with a whitish foamy film clinging to his teeth, he growled at the mirror. He leaned in so close that the mirror started to fog up.

He's lost his mind, I thought.

Exeter licked the steam off the mirror and growled again. A little voice in my head suggested that I pull out my transporter and silently sneak up on him. My mouth, however, had different plans. Before I realized what I was doing, I blurted out, "Wh-what are you doing?"

"No," said a voice behind me. "The question is, What are *you* doing?"

I turned around. It was my brother, Harold.

He started to push open the bathroom door. "Out of the way, weenie."

I grabbed the door and stood in the doorway, blocking his way. My heart started pounding. "You don't want to come in here," I blurted. There was no way I could explain another me in the bathroom, let alone an alien-imposter me who was dipping my brother's toothbrush in the commode and swallowing all of his pimple cream.

"Why not? Afraid I'm going to see the imaginary friend you were talking to?"

"I don't have an imaginary friend," I said.

"Right. Out of the way. I need to brush."

"You'd better use the bathroom downstairs," I said. Harold didn't budge.

"And the reason a worthless slime taco like you is telling a larger, older, clearly superior human being to use the other bathroom is . . . ?"

A list of excuses my brother might actually believe scrolled through my head. "Ummm . . . it smells really bad in here."

A growly noise came from the bathroom. I froze.

"What was that?" Harold asked.

"My stomach," I said. "I'm not feeling too good.

I've got the worst case of the farts. Really. Maybe you should use the other bathroom."

Harold gave me a look of utter and total disgust.

"What is *happening* to you, man?" he asked.

I shrugged.

"At least give me my toothbrush," he said. I slipped into the bathroom and slammed the door behind me. Exeter, grinning, wiggled Harold's toothbrush at me.

"Hey!" Harold called from the hallway.

"Just a miiiiiiinute, sweetie!" Exeter yelled back in a squeaky, girly voice.

"Shut up!" I hissed. I grabbed my own toothbrush, opened the door just enough to shove my hand through it, and tried to pass my toothbrush to Harold.

He didn't buy it.

"This is *your* toothbrush. Do you really think I want whatever disease is turning you into a one-man biological disaster?"

"Sorry," I yelled.

"Here you go!" Exeter yelled at almost the same time. He rubbed Harold's toothbrush in his armpit.

"Shhh!" I hissed.

"Are you telling *me* to be quiet?" Harold yelled, jamming his foot into the door so I couldn't shut it all the way. I leaned against the door so he couldn't open it any farther.

"No!" I said. "I was talking to myself!"

Exeter had an evil grin on his face and a white bubble of pimple cream at one corner of his mouth. I snatched the toothbrush out of his hand and handed it out the door.

"That's more like it," Harold said.

"Uh—uh . . . I gotta go. I think I'm having another attack!" I yelled. I pushed the door closed and locked it.

Once Harold's footsteps had faded away, I turned to Exeter and asked, "Are you completely insane?" He tilted his head like a dog listening to a command he didn't understand.

"Just having a little fun," he said.

"You *cannot* brush your teeth with toilet water and pimple cream! That's disgusting!"

"Right." Exeter waved his hand like this was entirely beside the point. "Whatever. You can't tell me it's any worse than squash casserole."

"Look," I said. "You can't stay here on Earth. You especially can't stay here in my house. Why don't you just go back to wherever it is that you're supposed to be and turn yourself in? I'm sure they'll go easy on you."

Exeter stared at me as if I had just suggested we enter a chicken-dance contest.

"Okay?" I asked.

Exeter continued to stare.

"Please?"

Exeter chuckled. "You're so cute when you beg. I love Earth. I love earthlings. I've watched all your shows. I've always wanted to see this place. Why should I leave? I even did a school project on Earth."

"No."

Exeter nodded.

"Really?" I asked.

He nodded.

"Like with some kind of special telescope or warp drive spaceship or something?"

"Actually," Exeter said, "I did a diorama."

"A diorama?"

He nodded proudly.

"You did a diorama. Oh, yeah, that's great." A headache had begun pounding behind my eyes. "You have space travel and giant talking squids and translators and Rigelian squash casserole and that's all you could come up with? A diorama? I did a diorama in second grade!"

"But it was a *cool* diorama," he said.

"Look," I said. "Can't you at least turn into someone else?"

"Nah. I don't feel like it. Not for another day or two," he said. "It takes a lot of energy. But don't mess with me." He assumed an odd sort of kung-fu pose. "I have powers." He bugged out his eyes and wiggled his fingers.

My mother called up the stairs. "Sam! Are you feeling all right, honey?"

"Fine!" I yelled through the bathroom door.

"Oh, really?" Exeter asked. "It's fine for me to stick around and be you for a while? Great!"

"No!" I whispered. "I wasn't talking to you!"

"Time to go, Sam!" Mom called.

"I'm coming!" I yelled.

"Here I come," Exeter yelled, imitating me. "I can't wait for school!"

I could hear my mom's footsteps as she started up the stairs.

"Shhh!" I said. I gave Exeter one more dirty look and stepped out of the bathroom.

"I'm ready," I said. "Let's go!"

"It's nice to see you so eager to go to school for a change," Mom said as we both headed downstairs.

I looked back as I got to the foot of the stairs and caught a glimpse of Exeter dashing out of the bathroom. He waved cheerfully as he vanished into my room.

Chapter Eight

Unfortunately school wasn't any safer than home. On my way through the lunchroom, Bradley stuck out his foot and tripped me. I landed on top of my tray, nose to nose with my fish sticks. Not a cool moment for me. A couple of girls sitting at the nearest table were laughing.

"Nice going, spaz," Bradley said. I picked up the tray and what was left of my lunch, and dumped it into a trash can nearby.

"Hey, aren't you going to sit with us?" his large friend asked as I walked by.

"Hey, dude!" Bradley said, leaning toward me. "You know, I'll tell you the cool new nickname we got for you."

"Yeah," his friend said. "Wanta hear it?"

"Not really," I said, and walked away.

Later in the hallway, Harold cornered me near my locker. "I heard about your doing a nosedive into your lunch today."

"Yeah."

"Why do you let those losers pick on you?"

"I can't help it if they're jerks," I said. "And I have other things on my mind."

"Well, then learn to focus. Tell them to take a hike. Seriously. You're embarrassing me. And I have an image to maintain. I'm telling you this for your own good."

"Fine."

"What do you mean, fine? Fine, you'll actually stand up for yourself? Or, fine, you'll be picking tuna surprise out of your hair for the rest of the year?"

"Fine, I'll handle it."

"Look," Harold paused to peer down the hallway. He really did look embarrassed to be seen with me. "I'm not saying you should try to beat this Bradley guy up. I mean, let's face it, the janitor would have to squeegee you off the wall. But you've got to find some way to stand up for yourself, okay?" For a moment he actually looked concerned.

The moment passed. "Because you are a disgrace to the family name," he added. "I swear, I'm gonna tell everyone we ordered you from the Sears catalog if you don't get it together."

I nodded. Harold combed his hair down in a way he thought looked good because it hid the pimples on his forehead, adjusted his collar, and glided away down the hall. He was not nearly as cool as he thought he was; but then again, I didn't have much to brag about myself.

Chapter Nine

I walked home from school and found trouble waiting in my driveway.

Right where the package had been sitting was Exeter, barefoot, wearing my mother's tennis visor backward and an old, faded "I'm with stupid" T-shirt, picking at his big toe.

I walked up to him. "Nice look," I said. He flicked away some sort of goop he'd scraped from under his toenail. "I really like the statement you're making here." He looked up at me. There was just a hint of something off-kilter in his eyes. "So does this work for you? Do you meet a lot of girls this way?"

Abruptly he stood up. "You're kind of sarcastic, aren't you?" he asked. He sounded mildly amused. "When you dare to speak, anyway."

I dropped my backpack at the edge of the driveway.

Exeter gave me a sour grin and said, "That's about all you've got going for you, though. You know, I've spent the day studying you. You have nothing cool in your room. You can't shape-shift, you don't have spines or tentacles or anything else neat like that, and I hate to mention it"—he smoothed his shirt and chuckled to himself—"actually, never mind. I kind of like reminding you, you're kind of short. Have you noticed this? Hmmm? No wonder nobody wants to hang out with you."

"It has nothing to do with spines," I said. "Tentacles. Whatever."

"Oh, really?" Exeter said. "Then how do you explain the fact that you have no friends?"

"I just moved here," I said, "and I made sort of a bad first impression. Sometimes it takes people a while to find out who you really are."

"Which would be a total loser. You know, it's a good thing I came along to rescue your life from dullness. You need my help. You want to know what's really wrong with you?"

"Not really," I said. "I've gotten enough advice today." I was tired of discussing my life so I reached out to grab Exeter. The transporter was jammed in my pocket. He was standing right in front of me. How hard could it really be to send him back home?

Exeter grinned. "Not so fast," he said. And as he said it, an electrical tingle shot through my fingers where they were touching his shirt. He seemed to be giving off some sort of strange energy. For a moment I had an awful feeling in my mouth like I'd just bitten down on a hunk of aluminum foil.

Then everything was spinning around me. I heard a strange rushing in my ears, and the world went black.

Chapter Ten

When I came to, I was standing in some sort of strange, rocky place. Around me were foul-smelling brownish boulders.

Something warm and wet splattered over my head and shoulders. I looked up—and saw that I was staring directly into the giant snout of my dog, Hector. Another glob of drool fell from his mouth and splattered next to me like gooey, dog-breath-scented rain.

And then I realized where I was—sitting in Hector's food bowl, covered in drool, as he prepared to eat his dinner. I had been shrunk to the size of a bug—and was about to become dog chow.

It wasn't athletic ability that got me up and out of

there. It wasn't my new sneakers. It wasn't superior intelligence.

It was desperation—sheer, screaming desperation to get as far away as possible from Hector's drooling, chewing, completely oblivious mouth. I scrambled, frantically, as Hector's snout closed in, clawing my way through the kibble and over the edge of the bowl. He gave sort of a curious snuffle, but hardly paused. Nothing, but nothing, distracts Hector from his food, not even a roach-sized human hotfooting it out of his bowl.

Once I was out of range, I decided the first thing I needed to do was find an out-of-the-way place to hide and see what was going on. My mother had a pair of rubber boots sitting on the floor in a corner, and I settled down on top of one to wait.

I didn't have to wait long. Around the corner and into the kitchen came . . . me. Exeter was still wearing the "I'm with stupid" T-shirt and still looked exactly like me, except for his severely damaged fashion sense.

He opened the fridge, pulled out the milk jug, took off the top, and stuck it into his mouth. He spit out the top and stuck his nose into the milk jug and sniffed. "Hmmm," he said, lifting the jug up in front of his eyes. "Klim," he mumbled. He must have been reading the label backward. He took a drink out of the jug. "Klim's not bad." He left the milk sitting out on the counter.

"Mom hates that," I mumbled to myself. He burped loudly, scratched an armpit, then turned around to leave without closing the refrigerator door all the way. "Mom hates that, too," I said to myself.

Then he did the unthinkable. Standing there with cool fridge air wafting around him, he gave a contented sigh and began picking his nose. Vigorously.

"Oh no," I said. "Now I'm a public nose-picker."

I guess I said that a little too loudly, because he jumped and began looking around the kitchen—with one finger still embedded deep in his nose. I watched, frozen with some combination of fear and disgust—and then jumped myself as his eyes found me. He grinned. "There's my little buddy!" he said jovially. "I dropped you when I was grabbing a snack"—he motioned toward a box of dog treats—"and I thought I'd lost ya. Oh good. Now that you're short—I mean, even shorter than before— it's just a matter of time before you get squished by someone or other. But I was really hoping to be the one to do it."

He was only a few steps away. I wasn't sure where to run. It wouldn't do any good anyway. I was going to die at the hands of a nose-picking alien criminal. "Yikes," I said.

And then I was saved.

Just as Exeter spotted me, my brother walked into the kitchen.

"Whoa! You want some fries with that booger? Man, that is just gross," Harold said. "You know, I think you used up all your snot a couple of years ago, and now you're just reaching up there and picking out little pieces of brain."

Exeter removed his finger from his nose and gave Harold a nasty glare. I should have been running away, but for the first time in my life, I was enjoying Harold picking on me.

"Perhaps we should discuss this some other time," Exeter said, and leaned to the side, trying to keep me in view.

"Excuse me," Harold said. "But do I see you poking around in the refrigerator with your slime-coated, snot-infested hands? Do you realize that the rest of us have to eat that food, too? If you touched any of last night's pizza with those crud-covered hands, I will be forced to beat you senseless."

Exeter turned around, reached into the fridge, grabbed a slice of pizza, and proceeded to blow his nose onto it.

I should be taking notes, I thought. This guy really knows how to give Harold the business.

And with that Harold swung his fist. Exeter ducked and started to step around him but tripped over one of Harold's extremely large feet, and fell, tripping Harold, too, in the process. They both tumbled to the kitchen floor with a thud and began rolling around and whaling on one another.

At this point I was laughing so hard that I couldn't stand up straight. I wasn't even sure whom to cheer for, although it looked like Harold was getting the upper hand. Alien or not, Exeter just wasn't as big as my older brother.

But then Exeter did something I haven't tried since I was two. He bit Harold.

I'm embarrassed to admit I was still laughing. There was something so demented and childish about it.

Howling in pain, Harold ripped his arm out of Exeter's mouth. Exeter used that opening to grab a metal mixing bowl that had fallen onto the floor and whack Harold on the head with it. It made a sound like a gong.

"Hey!" Harold yelped. "What's wrong with you? Little punk!" For a moment, he almost looked like he was going to cry. Then both of them burst into action again, kicking and punching. Now my brother seemed to be getting the worst of it.

The problem was, Harold was still holding back, trying not to really hurt the deranged creature he thought was me. But Exeter was going for blood. As they rolled over, I caught a glimpse of Exeter's face. His mouth was twisted into a vicious grin. And although Harold still had a handful of his shirt, he was edging toward the kitchen counter.

Edging toward the knives sitting on the kitchen counter.

My heart froze for a moment.

"No!" I screamed. Before I realized exactly what I was doing, I ran over to them as fast as I could move. I climbed onto Harold's head, narrowly avoided being whacked by Exeter's flailing hand, and leaped from Harold's head to Exeter's collar. I hoisted myself up, then found myself falling. Harold was howling again, and the two of them had rolled over.

With a *thup!* I slid over Exeter's chin and suddenly was lodged up to my waist in what felt like a warm, damp cave. I looked around, trying to get my bearings. In a flash I realized that Exeter was lying on his back, and Harold was sitting on top of him, still screaming.

And—horror of horrors—I was stuck, feet down, in one of Exeter's nostrils.

Before I could do anything about my situation, though, I had to help my brother. Behind Harold's back, I could see the knives, dangerously close to us.

"Harold!" I yelled as loud as I could. "Watch out!"

Harold stopped howling for a moment and leaned in closer to look at Exeter's face. "What the—"

I cringed as Exeter made a sort of angry growling noise.

"You jerk!" I yelled, and without really thinking—once again—I did the only thing that came to mind. I bent myself up toward the tip of Exeter's nose and bit it as hard as I could.

Exeter shrieked.

The next thing I saw was a split-second view of his dirty fingernail, whipping toward me. Then I was flying through the air. He had flicked me clean out of his nose, and I was hurtling through the kitchen.

I'm going to die, I thought. I am going to be splattered into ketchup when I land.

As I soared through the air, I curled up into a sort of ball, wrapping my arms around my legs.

And then it happened.

There was a flash of light and then a dizzying lurch, and suddenly I wasn't flying through my kitchen anymore.

Now I was flying through the office waiting room—up, over the squid-secretary, past the desk, and into the row of chairs filled with students. I slammed into Mixto, knocking him backward and sending his chair skidding away.

There was a moment of silence after I landed. I looked down and realized I was sitting on top of Mixto, who was flat on his back, looking dazed. "You okay?" I asked. I was very relieved to be alive and back to my normal size.

Scattered on the floor were little yellow things that looked like Tic Tacs. I picked one up. "Breath mint?" I asked.

Then there was a hissing noise, and we were

enveloped in a foul yellow mist that smelled like a horrible combination of liver and onions, sweat socks, and cheap perfume. "No," Mixto gasped. "Stinking fog capsule." Then he rolled all six of his eyes up into his head and passed out.

Chapter Eleven

It was the squid-secretary who evacuated us with a slimy tentacle wrapped around both our necks (which gave me the chills) and silently, disapprovingly, escorted us back to the line of seats in the office once the smoke had cleared. She was glaring at us so intently that I was surprised we didn't burst into flames.

Once she had returned to her desk, I leaned over and whispered, "My gosh, Mixto! Why are you still here?"

Mixto squeezed all six of his eyes shut, then opened them one by one, starting on the far right. "They've been kind of busy around here."

"Sorry."

"Don't worry about it," he said. "They have a tendency to do this. I heard about this one kid who spent a year and a half waiting here in the chairs. There's a plaque over there with his name on it." He tilted his head toward the far wall, where a dusty bronze square hung. On the chair below it were what looked like a pillow, a blanket, and a half-eaten box of cookies.

I noticed the squid-secretary was glaring at us again, so I settled back in my chair and tried to look innocent. Mixto did the same.

A few minutes later after a couple of muted discussions over the intercom, she motioned to me with a tentacle. "Proceed to Miss Tyrell, Room 22B. Out the door, take a left, third door on your left. Do not stop to talk with any students." She fixed Mixto with a nasty look. "Go directly there."

"Ma'am?"

She sighed. "Yes?"

"I'm sorry about my, uh, accident. With the transporter. I'm sure it won't happen again."

She nodded impatiently.

"But I was wondering—something very odd happened to me—"

She cut me off with an impatient wave of a tentacle. "I have evaluations to type and test results to file, and the inspector's due at any minute."

"But—"

"Miss Tyrell. Out the door to your left, third door on the left."

"But—"

"Thank you," she said sternly, and turned back to her typing.

"Great," I muttered, turning to leave.

"Psst!" Mixto hissed, as I walked past his chair. He was staring straight ahead, not making eye contact. His lips barely moved when he spoke. "The janitor! Don't worry about Tyrell. Just ask the janitor."

"Ahem!" said the squid-secretary. "Out the door, turn to the left—"

"Third door on the left," I said, walking out into the hall.

Chapter Twelve

"Repeat after me: I am somebody."

"I am somebody," I said for the fourteenth time.

"Repeat: I feel good about myself."

I groaned. "I feel good about myself."

"All right now," said my new instructor, Miss Tyrell, the school guidance counselor. She was tall and skinny and constantly smiling, with a nose like a beak and hair pulled back into the tightest bun I had ever seen. The only thing not quite human about her was her chameleonlike skin, which was speckled green at the moment. "Are you thinking positively now?"

I smiled weakly. I was starting to nod off.

"Because if a puny human like you isn't thinking positive, constructive thoughts, he'll simply be turned into a boneless, foul-smelling bucket of slime by something as powerful as a Buterian mutant," she said. The smile never left her face. "So you need to think positive," she crooned.

"And of course you're going to have to fight dirty," she added in her cheerful kindergarten-teacher voice. And with that she turned an alarming shade of orange and yanked the chair out from under me. She tossed the chair into the air, split it in half with some sort of karate kick, and slammed the two broken chunks into the corner of the room. One of them bounced off a desk, causing a landslide of what looked like fill-in-the-bubble test forms.

"Ma'am?" I figured it was important to be polite to any alien with martial-arts skills. "I'm normal size again now. But I was tiny—bug-sized. What happened?"

She heaved a big sigh and returned to a grassy shade of green. "Didn't they prepare you at all? Buterian mutants have certain—skills. They can alter their own size and shape, and they can change the size and shape of other creatures, too. It doesn't work for long, but it can still cause problems."

"But how do I stop him from doing it again?"

She sighed impatiently. "You need to capture

and transport him quickly. Catch him by surprise. Distract him a little. You know, it's hard work to alter the size of another creature, even a relatively diminutive one like you. If you distract him, he won't be able to concentrate well enough to do it."

"But how do I distract him?"

She sighed again. "Oh, good heavens! Whatever works. Sing a song. Do a dance."

"Oh, that sounds like a great idea," I said. "I have to take time out from saving the world to put on a disco show."

She fluttered a hand in the air and a flush of turquoise dots spread over her. "Remember, now! Think positive. And don't forget that Buterians have very, very sensitive ears. Once he assumes his own shape, if you can grab him by the ears, he'll do whatever you want. Just make sure you get a good grip."

There was a knock on the door. Miss Tyrell looked at her watch. "Well, it looks like we're out of time. The inspector will be here any minute, so you need to be on your way. We're trying to handle this situation . . . discreetly."

"Yes ma'am," I said. "I swear, when this is all over, I won't tell anyone about any of this."

"You won't tell any other humans?" She laughed,

turning a merry shade of pink. "Oh, go ahead, dear. It's not the humans I'm worried about. Tell *them* all you want." Miss Tyrell patted my cheek. "They'll never believe you anyway."

"But—"

She smiled gently and pushed the button on my transporter for me. "There you go, dear!"

Chapter Thirteen

Miss Tyrell's lecture must have taken longer than I realized because by the time she zapped me back home, my house was dark and silent. I checked the clock in the kitchen: 5:30 A.M.

I tiptoed up to my room. Harold's door was ajar. I peeked in. He was sprawled on his bed, surrounded by open books, empty chip bags, and banana peels. He seemed fine.

The door to my room was shut. Slowly and quietly I turned the knob. If Exeter was in there, I could surprise him.

There was a lump in the bed. I took a deep breath. "Go for the ears," I whispered to myself. Then I pounced.

And let me tell you, the pillow and pile of dirty

clothes mounded under my covers never had a chance. I got them in an amazing, pro-wrestling-quality stranglehold.

Unfortunately that's all there was—just clothes. No Exeter under the covers, or under the bed, or in the closet.

I was poking my laundry hamper with a Wiffle-ball bat when I heard a *scritch-scritch-scritch* at my door. I froze.

"Sam? Are you up already?"

My dad was standing in the hallway, looking a little dazed. He always looked strange to me when he wasn't wearing his glasses.

"Couldn't sleep," I said.

"I heard thumping," he said.

"Sorry."

"Right," Dad said. He stood at the doorway for a moment, then wobbled into my room and sat down on the bed. "Way too early."

I nodded.

"Couldn't sleep, huh? Upset about yesterday?"

Uh-oh, I thought. I shrugged.

Dad yawned. "Well, I guess you should be. Quite a day."

I nodded.

"You know, I'm used to you smarting off once in a while. But all of this fighting—is there something you need to tell me about?"

My heart sank. What on Earth had Exeter been doing?

"And the mayonnaise . . .," Dad said. "I didn't think you even *liked* mayonnaise."

He looked at me, clearly expecting some kind of answer. I was starting to feel a little sick to my stomach.

"Well . . . I haven't been myself lately," I said. "Just the move . . . and stuff."

"Stuff?"

"You know—school. Homework. Global warming. World peace. Killer mutant space aliens." I sneaked a look at Dad's face. He still looked half asleep. Clearly he wasn't considering the possibility that a rampaging mutant had taken over his son's life.

"Right," he said. "The usual." He rubbed his eyes. "You'll let me know if it's anything more serious?"

I nodded. "Don't worry, Dad. You'll definitely know about it."

Dad nodded vaguely. "Mmmm-hmmmm." He

patted me on the head and yawned. "So you think we can both go back to bed now?"

"I guess so," I said.

He slowly walked out of the room.

I lay back on my bed, my brain racing through the possible disasters Exeter had caused in my life. What on Earth had he done? I closed my eyes, just for a moment, trying to concentrate.

The next thing I heard was my mother banging on my door and yelling, "You are absolutely not sleeping in this morning, mister! You have fifteen minutes to get ready, and then I am taking you to school even if you're still in your pajamas!"

Chapter Fourteen

"What do you have to say for yourself?" my mother asked, pointing at me with a spatula.

"Ummmm. Uh." I wasn't exactly feeling light on my feet this morning. "Sorry?"

"You're darn right, sorry," she said. "Really, Samuel."

"Mmmmfff!" my dad said emphatically from behind his newspaper.

"What I said last night still goes, young man," Mom said.

"Uh-huh?" I said.

"You're grounded for two weeks. You go to school, you come home, and that's it. Nothing else." I took a chance on looking her in the face, in the hope of figuring out exactly how much trouble I was in.

Apparently a lot.

"Don't give me your innocent look," she said. "I will not have you fighting with your brother. Not in this house. How could you bite him like that?"

I shrugged.

"And I don't know what sort of weird prank that was, eating an entire jar of mayonnaise. And taking apart the blender. And blaming the dog for that long-distance call I caught you making. Really, Sam."

Harold looked up from his cereal. He was fighting back a smile. "Well, I let the dog *dial* it," he said in a cheesy falsetto, obviously imitating me. "How was I supposed to know he'd call Albania?"

"That's enough from you," Mom said, "unless you want to be grounded, too."

"That's not fair!" Harold said. "I actually *have* a social life for you to mess up."

"Oh, Harold," Mom said. She sounded completely out of patience. "I get the distinct feeling you've been egging him on. I've had enough of that, too."

"*Mmmm-hhhmmff,*" my dad added. Then he got up, kissed my mom on the cheek, gave Harold a playful punch on the shoulder, and patted me on the head on his way out of the kitchen. He is not a morning person, even when he *has* had a full night's sleep.

I had just enough time to grab a piece of toast before Mom shooed me and Harold out the door, too. "Come on," she said. "You're late. I'll drop you at school, but you have to come right now, or you'll make me late for work." As she herded me along, I turned and looked back—just in time to see Exeter peeking around the stair landing, wearing one of my dad's ties around his head like a bandanna.

"Let's go!" my mother yelled, grabbing me by the elbow. I didn't have any choice. I went.

All the way to school, I wondered what horrible things Exeter would do next. It was a good thing my parents had left for work, I guess. Otherwise I would have spent the day worrying that he was going to barbecue them while I was at school. He could have my brother, though.

Chapter Fifteen

"So do you want to know what your nickname is?" Bradley asked.

I examined my cold hamburger.

"Hey!" Bradley said, sitting down across from me. "Are you listening?"

I was sitting next to a guy named Rob who I sort of knew from my English class. He looked over at me and rolled his eyes. "Did *you* hear anything?" Rob asked me.

"What?" I said. "I can't seem to hear anything."

"Hey!" Bradley said, and poked Rob in the arm. "Do *you* want to know?"

I took one last look at my hamburger then

dropped it on my plate. I wasn't hungry anyway. "Leave him alone," I said.

Rob shrugged. "It's not a big deal."

The bell for class rang. Bradley reached over, grabbed my hamburger, and took a big bite. Then he held his hand to his ear. "Oh, dear, is that the bell? I must fly away! I wouldn't want to be late." He grinned at me, still chewing. Little pieces of hamburger swam around in his mouth.

Rob made a face. "You should get that fixed," he said. He turned to me. "Gotta go to class. You coming?"

"Yeah," I said. As I stood up, Bradley grabbed the English book sitting next to my tray and hurled it into the wall. A couple of papers fell out, and the front cover, which had barely been hanging on, ripped off and slid under a table.

"Nice," Rob said.

"Go ahead," I said. "I'll get it." It was too embarrassing to have what may be my only friend watch me crawl around the cafeteria. Rob shrugged and turned to leave. Bradley laughed and walked away with a piece of hamburger meat wedged in the corner of his mouth. On the way out of the cafeteria, he high-fived one of his friends.

I collected the assorted pieces of my English book. A teacher I didn't know walked over and asked, "Everything all right here?"

"Oh, yeah," I said. "Everything is great."

Chapter Sixteen

After school I went straight home, searched the house, and found—nothing. Yet again.

So I stretched out on the couch for a moment. What could Exeter be doing?

As I lay there I decided to start my search in the garage, then work my way through the house, top to bottom. I sat up, determined to launch my own counterattack.

And that's when the trouble began.

Exeter was standing across the room from me, grinning wickedly. It looked like he was holding my dad's electric razor, except that he had attached a couple other gizmos to it. One of them was an old TV remote. The other looked like part of a blender.

I should be terrified, I thought, but I wasn't. Mostly I was just very, very curious. "Now what?" I asked.

"Oh, this is just a little something I whipped up while you were at school. An antigravity unit. Isn't it cool? I think I can have a lot of fun with this."

"So you're gonna do *what* with that? Float around like an astronaut? So what?"

Exeter smiled. "Oh, it's not me who's going to be bouncing around. It's you. One shot, and you'll be floating."

"So? That sounds kind of cool."

"Maybe. Until you get tired. Or fall asleep. Or just get pushed a little too hard. Then off into the sky. Off into outer space. Bye-bye. And I can take over your life completely. Hey, maybe I'll take over the whole planet, too." He had a rapturous look on his face.

I wasn't sure I felt up to this, but I couldn't stall any longer. Now was my chance. I tensed up, about to jump him—and he flipped the switch on his device. A wavering beam of light shot out of it, hitting my shirt. For a moment I was enveloped in a pinkish light. My clothing felt hot and prickly, as if it were made of electrified Brillo pads. Then Exeter's device made a loud buzzing noise and started smoking. He whacked it a couple of times, grumbling, and it shorted out.

"Worthless human trash," he said. "Can't even get decent components for an antigrav unit here. When I take over I am definitely fixing that." He turned and walked out of the room. As he left he called over his shoulder, "You wait here. I'll be back to finish you off."

Which was the last thing I planned on doing, except that I couldn't move.

Chapter Seventeen

I could lift my head, at least a little, but my chest felt like an elephant was sitting on it. My legs seemed to weigh as much as tree trunks. As hard as I tried, I couldn't sit up. In fact I couldn't seem to budge myself off the couch at all. Exeter's device had done *something* to me. But what was it?

I must have lain there on the couch, feeling like a stranded whale, for almost an hour, until my mother got home from work.

"There's no reason for you to leave your jacket lying on the floor," she said. "I want you to go hang it up. And for that matter I want those dirty clothes in your room put into the hamper, not strewn all over the floor."

I tried to say something, but all that came out was a sort of weak gurgling sound.

"Really, Samuel, you'd think your clothes weighed a ton the way you drop them all over the place. I think you can find the strength to put them where they belong."

I nodded weakly. My mother harrumphed, gave me one of those mother looks, and walked out of the room.

Then I realized—hey, my mother is a genius! That was exactly the problem. Exeter's malfunctioning device must have done something to my clothing because it felt like it was made out of solid rock. The stuff weighed a ton. Until I got rid of it, I wasn't going anywhere.

After a few minutes of pointless effort, I realized I needed a plan. Lying on the couch didn't do me any good. I needed something to hook my shirt on so I could squirm out of it. With a painful thud, I rolled onto the floor. Rolling, I discovered, was a much easier way to move, especially since I couldn't bend my arms or legs very well.

Eventually I managed to snag my shirt collar on the edge of a magazine rack. It probably took me ten minutes to inch myself out of the shirt. Once my arms were free, getting out of my jeans wasn't that hard, although I got tangled up because I forgot to take my shoes and socks off first.

Then—I was free. I was naked. And I was staring directly at my brother, Harold, and his friend Mike, who had just walked into the living room.

Harold just stared at me. "I should probably beat you up," he said, "but I'm not sure it would do any good."

Mike shook his head. "Man," he said. "I think your brother needs some help."

They both turned and walked upstairs.

It was time for me to get to work. Job one: finding some clothes that wouldn't turn me into human Jell-O. I decided to check the laundry room, but had only made it as far as the kitchen when the front door slammed. I grabbed the first thing I could find—a "Kiss the Cook" apron hanging on the pantry door—and tied it around my waist. So much for dignity.

Exeter appeared in the kitchen doorway. He was back—still looking exactly like me, except fully dressed. After one glance at me, he started laughing. I seized my opportunity and lunged at him, grabbing him by the ear.

He kept laughing. He didn't care.

Then he got mean. He reached around behind him and grabbed a spatula off the counter with one hand and a wooden spoon with the other. *Whack!* He smacked me on the head with the spoon. I let go of his ear and tried to shield my head. *Thwap!* He slapped the spatula against my ribs and started poking me in the stomach with the spoon handle.

He grabbed my arm. "I'm going to shrink you back to bug size, then I'm gonna stomp you into jam." He wrinkled his forehead. He seemed to be concentrating very hard.

So I did the only thing I could do. I began to boogie.

"Oh, baby, baby," I sang, doing a sort of spastic hula dance.

Exeter looked utterly appalled. "If you could see yourself, you would be so ashamed," he said. He gripped my arm even tighter. I danced harder. The wrinkles on his forehead deepened. He squeezed his eyes shut.

"Oh, baby, baby," I sang. "Having a little trouble concentrating? Wooo-hooo! Yeah!"

His eyes popped open again. He leaned forward and screamed, *"I am going to kill you!"* I started laughing. I couldn't help it.

Then he grabbed my mother's electric hand mixer, turned it on, and charged toward me, aiming the whirling beaters at my head.

I ran for it.

A second later the mixer's cord popped out of the wall, and I heard a crash as the mixer—and probably Exeter, too—clattered to the floor.

I would have been fine, but before I could re-group, I tripped over the pair of jeans I'd left lying on the living-room floor and slammed down face-first onto the carpet.

I'd forgotten about the transport device jammed into my pocket. When I fell I must have whacked it with my knee, and you probably know what hap-pened next.

It was bad enough to land facedown on the squid-secretary's desk, wearing nothing but a "Kiss the Cook" apron, but what made it worse was that it must have been her lunch break.

My crash landing sent a bowl careening across the room. A cup of what smelled a little like coffee mixed with bowling-alley shoe deodorizer splattered over my feet. I ended up with the remains of some sort of sandwich smeared in my hair, and it looked like I had sent a full plate of squash casserole sailing onto the squid-secretary's lap. The only thing on her desk that escaped the carnage was her little intercom.

Without even pausing to wipe the squash off her eyeglasses, she leaned on the button and snarled, "Director? There's someone here to see you again."

Chapter Eighteen

It's hard to do push-ups when a giant lizard is rest-ing his foot on your back. It's even harder when he's yelling insults at you.

"Miserable scaleless weakling!" Axolotl shouted. "Cowardly shrunken mammal! Wretched non-egg-laying mucous bag!"

After forty push-ups and a lot more insults, I suddenly found myself staring directly at a pair of neatly shined shoes. I looked up—and saw they were attached to Miss Tyrell, who was a sunny shade of yellow. She shook her head disapprovingly. "Poor dear," she said.

"Really, Axolotl," she said, turning to him with her hands on her hips. "Don't you think this is a bit much?"

"Humans!" he sputtered. "No self-discipline! He's going to fail!"

"Shhh!" Miss Tyrell hissed as blue speckles spread over her arms. In a loud whisper she said, "You'll upset the poor dear."

"You know," I interrupted, "if you don't think I'm right for the job, it's fine with me if you send someone else. I mean, I wouldn't be insulted or anything. I'm just not that good at confrontations."

"Don't be silly," Miss Tyrell said. "You'll do fine—you just haven't been properly prepared."

"And whose fault is that?" Axolotl asked.

"Yours," she said. "Apparently the human never even knew how to return Exeter to his original shape."

"*You* could have mentioned that, too, you know," Axolotl said.

"It was so basic, I was certain you'd already covered it." Miss Tyrell snorted. Brilliant purple dots popped up on her face.

"I was in a hurry! I had tests to grade. Anyway, it was right there on the board!" Axolotl yelped, gesturing toward the wall. As he did he accidentally caught the little cord attached to Miss Tyrell's glasses. The glasses went flying across the room.

Miss Tyrell gave a gasp of outrage and turned dark orange. Axolotl suddenly looked terrified. "It was—I just—I'm so—" he said, backing up. She reached out and grabbed him by the nose, then yanked him forward. He tripped over me and went sprawling across the floor. I scuttled out of the way.

Axolotl hopped back up. His feet squeaked against the floor like sneakers during gym class. "Now I think maybe you're overreacting, Gladys. I didn't mean to do that. It was just a little—"

Miss Tyrell cut him off in midsentence with a giant leaping kick to the chest. She landed on top of him, looking rather embarrassed to be sitting on top of a giant lizard. She bumped her head on a cabinet as she tried to get up, and Axolotl chuckled. "Serves you right," he said.

With that she got an angry glint in her eyes and a case of red spots. She paused, glaring at Axolotl, her spots glowing. Then she pounced.

They launched into full-scale battle, rolling across the floor and making angry squalling noises like a couple of cats.

They seemed to have forgotten me entirely. "Excuse me," I said. I watched for another minute, then edged over to the desk, picked up a new transporter, readjusted my apron, and headed out the door. Apparently my briefing was over.

I walked down the hallway, back toward the director's office, trying not to attract too much attention. Apparently a human in a "Kiss the Cook" apron was not really that exciting a sight because most of the students didn't even look my way.

In fact the only person who seemed to notice me at all was the janitor, who winked at me. That wouldn't have surprised me, except that his eyelids didn't close up and down like mine—they closed sideways, like a pair of curtains. Very sophisticated alien curtains.

The director had warned me, when all this started, not to discuss my . . . problem . . . with other aliens at the school. But then again, up to this point I hadn't gotten very far by following directions. And hadn't Mixto suggested I talk to him?

The janitor leaned on his broom and smiled at me. "So you're wondering how to catch a Buterian mutant, I hear," he said, and chuckled. "Ahhh, the adventures of the young. You know, when I was not much older than you, I got into a fight with three of 'em. Quite a mess to clean up afterward." He sighed. "Those were fine days. Very fine days."

"Everybody here claims they're trying to help, but they never seem to tell me what I really need to know," I said. "I'm not sure they *want* me to know. They don't seem to be in any hurry to get this Exeter guy back."

The janitor grinned. He had a lot of teeth. "The folks around here get a little uptight during tests and inspections. They have trouble thinking about anything else."

I thought about the giant piles of papers and booklets in my own school's office. I guess that's true everywhere in the universe.

"So what do you recommend?" I asked.

"Buterians can be pretty difficult to deal with, but there are a whole variety of chemical compounds that can force them to return to their original shape, at least for a few minutes. Most of the compounds are a little too . . . volatile . . . for a human to carry around. But I know of one that you're sure to have lying around your house somewhere."

I leaned forward. "Carnauba wax," the janitor said. "Just a little dab will do it." He leaned toward me and whispered another suggestion in my ear.

He winked again. "But you'd better be moving

along. The director will be coming around the corner in a few seconds."

"How do you know all this?" I asked, not sure I really believed him.

"Janitors," he said, "know everything."

And with a little flourish of his broom, he stepped into an empty classroom, just as the director rounded the corner.

Chapter Nineteen

For a few seconds I was happy. I'd been zapped back to Earth again, landing right on my own bed, and everything seemed to be normal.

Then my door creaked open. Exeter leaned in. "Shhh," he whispered, holding his finger to his lips. "Let's not make a scene." He held up his device, which was now wrapped in duct tape and had a piece of a TV antenna attached to it. Then without another word, he zapped me.

"Sam, dear," my mother called from downstairs. "Can I see you for a minute? I have to run next door. . . ."

"Sure thing," Exeter called in a sickly sweet voice, and vanished.

I had been a bit startled when he zapped me, but

now I felt fine. In fact I felt great. It must not have worked, I thought.

Then I got out of bed.

All I did was roll over gently, then sort of push myself up so I was sitting. But that was all it took. I found myself rocketing through the room, slamming into the wall, spinning in midair, then bouncing against the ceiling. What finally stopped me was that my foot got tangled up in a mobile of the planets hanging from the ceiling. I hung upside down, swaying slightly.

He'd actually done it. He'd gotten rid of something so basic I'd never really thought about it until it was gone: gravity.

Despite the fact that I was in trouble with strange aliens who thought I was a complete idiot, my family thought I had lost my mind, and an interplanetary impersonator was walking around, pretending to be me, I had to admit that at this moment my life was very, very cool.

It probably took me at least twenty minutes to actually put on a shirt and a pair of jeans. (In zero-g, a "Kiss the Cook" apron doesn't provide a lot of coverage.) But I got dressed while doing a bunch of flips in midair, which is a lot more entertaining than my usual wardrobe experience.

My first goal was a simple one—find my secret weapon.

Future students of chemistry take note: Carnauba wax is found in virtually every product ever made. Candy. Those fruit gummy things. Car wax.

And luckily for me, my mother's makeup case.

At least that's what the janitor had whispered in my ear: "Just try lipstick."

Since I was already upstairs, I made my way to my parents' room and snagged the first tube of lipstick I saw—Luscious Passion Fruit Medley. Then I began the search for my nose-picking alien imposter.

Traveling in zero-g is actually fun, although I was accumulating a lot of bruises. All you have to do is push off against something stable—the wall, for instance—and glide. Of course if you push off a little crooked, you'll start to twist around in midair, so instead of gracefully finding a handhold and stopping yourself, you'll gracefully slam your nose against the banister or gracefully whack a hanging spider plant with your foot or gracefully get tangled in the chandelier. All of which I managed to do.

While I was gracefully thumping around the living room, Exeter was obviously up to something new. He was holding a clothes hanger, the cordless phone, a wad of aluminum foil, and a screwdriver.

He grinned up at me. "If you think my antigrav unit was cool, wait'll you see what I have in store for your planet now." He paused to jam his finger up his nose.

Exeter was out of control. Obviously I couldn't wait any longer. Wrenching my foot loose, I kicked off against the ceiling as hard as I could, hurtling through the air toward Exeter, holding a tube of Luscious Passion Fruit Medley out in front of me.

With a cry of triumph, I whipped the lipstick back and forth like Zorro with his sword. Victory was in my hands—until he leaped aside at the last moment, and my brave attack became an unprovoked assault on a defenseless couch.

With little slashes of Luscious Passion Fruit Medley all over it, the couch even looked a little as if it was bleeding. I pushed off from the couch as quickly as I could. I had to stop Exeter before he ran out the door. I couldn't handle the zero-g thing outside without eventually finding myself drifting through outer space.

This time I got lucky. Almost immediately I slammed into Exeter's back, knocking him over. More streaks of lipstick, this time on the carpet. He rolled over, grabbed my legs, and tried to toss me toward a window. I grabbed his hair with my free hand. Instead of flying away from him, I circled around him, still holding his hair, swinging around like a tetherball.

Then I lost my grip and slammed into the wall. Exeter was holding his head and howling. When I looked down at my free hand, I realized I was holding a handful of hair. A big handful.

Gripping a windowsill, I got ready to launch myself at Exeter before he could try to escape again. His eyes narrowed to slits—he wasn't thinking about getting away anymore, he was thinking about revenge. And I started thinking that maybe I should be armed with something a little more powerful than lipstick.

But there wasn't a lot of time for me to worry about it. With a snarl Exeter leaped at me, his eyes glowing with fury. I had no idea my own face could look so ferocious. I held the Luscious Passion Fruit Medley in front of me like a sword. There didn't seem to be anything else I could do.

For a moment I thought I was a goner. Teeth

scraped my neck and hot, oniony breath blew in my face. Then suddenly everything and everyone seemed to freeze, like a videotape put on pause. Exeter was frozen in midbite. The tube of lipstick was stuck in his left ear and seemed to be sending off sparks.

Then everything unfroze. Exeter fell to the floor, and I fell, too. Gravity. I sat up, rubbing my head where I'd whacked it on a potted plant. Exeter just lay on the floor, giving off a sound sort of like the air rushing out of a balloon. Then with a *pop*, he transformed.

There before me on the floor was the terror of the galaxy, the nose-picking alien menace who threatened the safety of Earth and every other solar system in the vicinity, the foul beast who was ready to reduce me to a pile of human goo.

He was a cute, little, pink, fuzzy bunny.

Chapter Twenty

"I want an explanation, and I want it now!"

My mother tightened her grip on my ear. I looked at the walls, the couch, and the floor, all festooned with vivid pink slashes of lipstick. I was covered with it, too—including the arms I had wrapped around Exeter the killer bunny. I had one of his ears clenched in my fist and didn't dare let go.

"Sam!" my mother shouted. "That was *not* a rhetorical question."

"Ummmm . . . art project?" I said. It was all I could think of.

My brother walked into the living room and immediately began snickering at me. "Whatever this is, I had nothing to do with it," he said. "I have no idea what's going on in his undersized brain."

"I don't know what you think is so funny, mister," my mom said. "You're his older brother. You are supposed to be keeping an eye on him. How exactly could you fail to notice him rampaging through the house?" She sneezed. "And you know I'm allergic to rabbit fur. I don't know where this guy belongs or how he ended up bright pink, which is not exactly a normal color for a rabbit, may I remind you. But you"—she pointed to Harold—"are going up to your room right now and you"—she gave my ear a painful yank—"are going to do something *responsible* with that rabbit and then get to work cleaning up this mess."

She looked really, insanely mad. So did Harold. Exeter the bunny, however, looked pretty content. Probably because he knew that I was facing something much more dangerous than black holes or cosmic rays: the wrath of Mom. I tightened my grip on his ear and squeezed him against my side with my arm. He actually seemed to be snuggling up against me. For a killer mutant he was pretty cute.

Mom sneezed again, then stomped off toward the kitchen. "I expect this place to be spotless," she called as she walked away. "And"—*achoo!*—"get rid of that rabbit!"

The cleanup might not be easy, I thought, but at least getting rid of Exeter will be. All I need is to click on the transporter to take him back and . . .

And where was my transporter, anyway?

Not in my pockets. Not on the floor. Not under the couch cushions. Rats. I put Exeter at the very top of a bookshelf and said, "Stay!" He wiggled his nose in a very adorable way.

Then I started hunting for the transporter in earnest. Not in the potted plant. Not under any of the living-room chairs. Not on the dining-room table. Not in the dog's bed.

Not anywhere, as far as I could tell.

Well at least I still had Exeter . . . somewhere. Out of the corner of my eye, I saw a flash of pink. How on Earth had he gotten down? He was hopping through the kitchen door. I raced after him—and saw another fleeting glimpse of pink as he vanished through the back door. I lunged for the door and tripped on the doorway, sliding painfully down the back-door steps nose first. Which gave me a great view of Exeter vanishing into my mother's rose bushes.

He was gone.

I was starting to wish I could vanish forever myself.

Chapter
Twenty-One

It took two hours to scrub the lipstick off the walls. A stain remover worked a little bit on the carpet, although it still looked faintly pinkish in some places. The couch left me stumped. Finally my mother just unzipped all the cushion covers that had been lipsticked and said she'd see if the dry cleaner could take care of them. She draped a sheet over the couch, gave me the evil eye, and sent me up to my room.

A little while later she brought me a peanut-butter-and-banana sandwich (I had scrubbed through dinner) and sat down next to me on the bed. "I don't really understand what was going on with you today," she said.

"Well," I sighed. There were times I suspected

my mother had a lie-detector death ray implanted in *her* head. "I was having sort of a lipstick fight with a friend, and we got a little carried away."

"What friend is this?" she asked.

"Umm . . . Exeter. He's a new kid in school."

"First of all, you're grounded. That means no friends coming over here. Second, next time take it outside. The living room is not a playground. Third, you need to find better ammunition than lipstick."

"Huh?"

"You know, if you're going to have a full-scale battle, go after each other with some serious artillery. Supersoakers. Mud. A giant bowl of mashed potatoes. And leave my lipstick out of it. Okay?"

"Okay."

She patted me on the head.

"I know you've been having a hard time lately," she said. "I *am* glad you've started making friends here. But seriously, you're going to have to keep it together, or you'll be grounded until you're thirty-five."

On her way out of the room, she added, "You haven't seen your father's electric razor lately, have you?"

I didn't sleep well that night.

The next day on the way to school, I stopped at the drugstore for eight tubes of the cheapest, ugliest lipstick I could find. I taped one tube to each ankle, put two in my front pants pockets, slipped two into my sleeves, stuck one in my back pocket and taped the last one inside a notebook. I was prepared this time. I was ready to meet my fate.

And my fate was definitely waiting for me.

Chapter Twenty-Two

For the very first time, I walked into Furniss J. Hotchkiss Middle School hoping the day would go by slowly. The longer school lasted the longer I'd have before my next encounter with Exeter. The longer I'd have until I was shrunk or made weightless or eaten for lunch. Bradley just didn't seem that bad by comparison.

Math class dripped by as slowly as ever. I spent most of the time trying to picture my teacher with tentacles instead of arms and wondering if I had time to slip into the bathroom between classes to practice my lipstick quick-draw.

English, however, was actually more interesting than usual.

"We are going to discuss poetry today," Mrs.

Barnett said, as a low, class-wide groan filled the room. "And you are all going to write your own haiku."

She started scribbling on the board. "Haiku is a type of short poem created by Japanese poets. It's a way of describing a particular time or place in just a few lines. It doesn't tell a story as much as it draws a sort of picture with words." She pointed to a little diagram on the board. "Five syllables for the first line, seven for the second line, five for the third line. Very simple."

"Very lame," Bradley muttered, and about half the class laughed.

"For those of you who are afraid of writing little three-line poems, I can always give you another assignment. Like a ten-thousand-word essay on appropriate classroom behavior."

The giggling stopped. Bradley looked sullen.

"Now," Mrs. Barnett said, "we have a whole page full of haiku to read today, but why don't we start by writing our own?" She sat on the edge of her desk. "Can someone suggest a first line? It has to be exactly five syllables, but it can be as many or as few words as you like. Even just one word, if you can think of one that fits."

The class fell silent. I was about to raise my hand

when a new chorus of laughter erupted from around Bradley.

"Mr. Michaels? Does that mean you have a suggestion for our poem?" Bradley glared at the teacher. "Let's have it."

"Boring poetry," he said. "That's five syllables, right?"

"Right," Mrs. Barnett said. "Now you're getting into the right spirit. Soon I bet you'll be spending all your spare time composing verse." She wrote "Boring poetry" on the board.

The class giggled.

"Anyone have a second line?" she asked. No one spoke. "Well, I suppose the rest of you are a bit stumped by the subject. How about I finish this one?"

She turned back to the blackboard and stood in front of it silently for a moment, then started writing. When she was done she stepped back, and we read the finished poem.

Boring poetry
Without it you will never
Pass grade number five.

"It's not exactly a work of art, but I think you get the point," Mrs. Barnett said. "And let me add that, despite the sentiments of the poem Mr. Michaels and I collaborated on, poetry does not have to be boring, as long as you're willing to use your brain a little. Let's see if all of you can come up with something a little more entertaining than this one."

We only had to write one, but by the end of class I had an entire page of them. My favorite was one I called "Summer Trip to the Grand Canyon." It had been the worst vacation of my life. It was not exactly an epic tale, but I thought it summed the experience up pretty well.

Mrs. Barnett walked around the room, reading what everyone had written. When she got to my desk, she paused and laughed. She tapped the summer trip one and said, "Very good. Mind if I read that one to the class?"

"I guess it's okay," I said.

She picked up my paper. "Now as proof that haiku isn't limited to chirping birds and whooshing waterfalls, I'll read you Sam's ode to a summer trip.

"Car with no a/c
Vacation meets disaster
Stuck to vinyl seats."

"Now that's only a dozen words, but it certainly gives you a pretty clear picture of what that trip was like, doesn't it? You can almost feel it, huh?" She handed the page back to me. "Nice work, Sam. Now does anyone else have one to share with the class?" She walked over to the other side of the classroom where a girl had raised her hand.

Rob, who was sitting next to me, slowly pulled his legs up off his chair with a sort of slurping sound, imitating the slow peel of legs stuck to vinyl. *"Shhhlupp. Shhhlupp.* Sounds just like my trip to New York. Thanks for reminding me." He grinned.

"Maybe we need to find a new travel agent," I said, and we both laughed.

Not a bad class, I thought as the bell rang. In fact, not such a bad day.

At least not until a few seconds later, when Bradley walked up behind me in the hallway and grabbed the sheet of poems out of my hand.

"Oooooo!" he squealed. "Let's see what we have here! Some sensitive poetry from a sensitive guy." His eyes skipped over the page, then stopped to rest on one of the poems. He stopped dead in the hallway, then bent over laughing. "Oh, this is too good."

His voice crept up to a falsetto, imitating Mrs. Barnett. "You see, class, poetry doesn't have to be about singing birds and whooshing waterfalls and bad vacations. It can be about class weirdos, too."

"Cut it out." I tried to grab the paper away from him, but all I managed to do was rip it.

Bradley held the paper over his head and started walking down the hall. When he was a few steps ahead of me, he held the page out in front of him and started reading one of the poems aloud.

"Pink, fuzzy bunny
Snarling, hissing jaws of death
Mutant imposter."

Bradley cackled with laughter. "Like it's not weird enough that he's afraid of pink bunnies, he had to write a poem about it." A couple of guys walking with him laughed. I ran a few steps to catch up, reached between them, and grabbed back the paper.

"Go ahead, take it, loser," Bradley said. "Add it to your scrapbook."

Any other day it might have been worth arguing with him. Any other day it might even have been worth a fight, although I would have gotten flattened.

But today—hearing him recite the bunny poem, even though I had actually written it as sort of a joke, had me feeling very jumpy. If only Bradley could lay off for just one day, just long enough for me to deal with Exeter. Obviously it was too much to ask.

Way too much. I slipped past him and walked away.

I made it through science and got to P.E. before disaster struck. I was in the locker room, changing into my gym clothes, when one of the tubes of lipstick slid out of my sleeve, bounced onto the floor, and rolled across the room. The guy standing next to me, Gibson, asked, "Hey, what was that?"

Then I heard Bradley. "Hmmm . . . someone seems to have lost something important." He turned around, stepped over the bench, and grinned at me. "Hey. . . . Lose something?" Gibson stepped back and gave me a puzzled look.

Great, I thought. As Bradley stepped closer, I jammed my jeans (three lipsticks in the pockets) into my locker and wrapped the other lipstick in my sleeve as I pulled my shirt off. One tube was buried under my clothes in a notebook, but he'd never think to look there.

"Well," Bradley said, sitting down next to me on

the bench. I was carefully rolling off one sock, letting the lipstick slide into the toe then jamming the bundle into my shoe. Bradley examined the label on the lipstick he'd picked up. "Hot Strawberry Kisses." He smiled. "Another fabulous fashion statement." His voice dropped to a loud whisper. "But maybe you don't want to wear your makeup during gym. Might smear it, you know."

Gibson laughed. How odd, I thought. Bradley's much funnier than usual. If it weren't me he was hassling, I might have laughed, too.

Bradley stood up and started poking through the pile of clothes in my locker. "Cut that out!" I said. I got up and pushed him away from my locker. Without really intending it, I slammed his hand holding the lipstick tube into the edge of my locker door, and he flinched and dropped the tube.

That was a mistake.

I am not exactly a champion boxer. I think I threw two punches, and I doubt either of them did any damage. To tell the truth, I wasn't really looking. I just started swinging when I saw him lunge at me.

Bradley was good, though. No wasted motion. He just punched me in the stomach, then tripped me. I was doubled over on the locker-room floor before there was even time for much of a crowd to gather.

As the class surrounded us, Bradley shoved me onto my stomach, sat on my back, and started to twist one arm behind my back. "You want to know why this looks so easy?" He laughed. "Because it is." I turned my head as far as I could, trying to look him in the face. It hurt to twist that far. "Whatcha looking at? Want to get up? But I was just getting comfortable." With one hand he twisted my arm even harder. He used his free hand to comb his hair back, then very casually began to pick his nose.

"Dude!" said someone in the crowd gathered around us. A couple of guys laughed. I looked up at Bradley, with his finger firmly embedded in his nose, thinking that this was pretty antisocial behavior even for him.

But not for Exeter.

The hair on the back of my neck stood up. This was bad—very, very bad.

Of course. I had gotten him pretty mad. What better way to torment me than to take on Bradley's shape?

My pondering was cut short by a shout from Coach Targis, who popped his head through the locker-room door. "Anyone who horses around in the locker room gets detention! Anyone who watches anyone horsing around in the locker room gets detention! Anyone who is not on the gym floor in five seconds gets detention!" Students began to bail out of the locker room. Exeter didn't budge. In seconds we were alone.

He grinned at me. It wasn't an ordinary grin. His teeth looked frighteningly sharp and white. A thin stream of drool trickled down his chin. I was in big trouble.

With a sudden wrench I tried to reach my free hand down to my sock where my one remaining tube of lipstick was hidden. But I couldn't move my arm far enough. "Looking for this?" Exeter asked, laughing, as he pulled the tube out of my sock then tossed it into one of the shower stalls.

He opened his mouth wide—wider than I thought a mouth could open—and his teeth glittered. He was about to attack. I was about to be ground into meat loaf. On a locker-room floor. By a nose-picking alien. It was not how I'd pictured the end.

Then Exeter and I both froze when we heard a voice at the doorway. "I have a note from the office, coach. I passed out after math. I'm not supposed to dress for gym."

"Well, go on in and get a drink of water if you want it," the coach said. "You can sit in the bleachers while the class plays ball."

And into the locker room walked Bradley—the real Bradley.

He saw us and stopped cold. His mouth opened but no sound came out. "I . . . I . . . What?" he finally croaked.

"As much as I'd like to hang around and enjoy this witty repartee, I have an earthling to destroy, a planet to conquer, and a luncheon I'd like to attend," Exeter said. "Why don't you run along?"

Bradley just stood there openmouthed, looking a little like a fish.

"No, wait," I said. Anything to buy a little time. "I wanted to ask you something."

Exeter gasped in mock surprise. "The meek and humble Sam speaks!"

I ignored him. "You said you had a nickname for me."

Bradley nodded. The rest of his body stayed

stock-still, except for one hand, which was fidgeting with his watch. He looked alarmed.

"Well?" I asked. "What is it?"

"Oh, nothing," Bradley whispered.

"Oh, come on," I said. "You've been dying to tell me. Right? Come on. Here's your big chance."

Exeter chuckled. "This should be good."

Bradley mumbled something.

"What?" Exeter and I asked.

"Spam," Bradley said.

"Spam," I repeated.

"Get it?" Bradley asked weakly.

"Sam the Spam . . . ," Exeter said in a tone of wonderment. "What's Spam?"

"That's it?" I said. "That's all you could come up with? All the garbage you've been giving me day after day, and that's it?"

"It rhymes," Bradley said.

"I caught that," I said. "I'll be sure to notify the Poetry Club."

Bradley managed a sickly smile. "Huh. Yeah."

"Kind of a letdown," Exeter said, looking as thoughtful as he possibly could, considering he had Bradley's face to work with. He heaved a disappointed sigh. "After I saw how worked up Sam the

Spam got about you, I thought you'd be a little more innovative than that."

Bradley stared blankly.

Exeter moaned. "You know, it was hard work tracking you down. I spent countless boring hours in conversation with Sam's worthless brother trying to get the goods on you."

"Hey—" I said.

Exeter twisted my arm a little harder. "Pipe down," he said. "I'll take care of you in a minute." He turned back to Bradley. "All the energy it took to assume your shape—utterly wasted. You turned out to be a nothing. A zero. An infinitely unworthy waste of protoplasm. At least Sam is kind of fun to mess with. But you are just a total loss." Bradley continued to stare blankly. "At least wave your arms or something so I know you're listening."

While Exeter launched into another series of insults, I saw my way out.

All the other lipstick tubes were far out of reach. But the one he'd been holding—the one he had picked up to taunt me with, then dropped by accident—had rolled over to the base of my locker. It was almost within reach. Almost.

"You are an overgrown lump with a brain the

size of an elementary particle," Exeter continued. "You have the intellectual capacity of a Mocktar slug with a severe headache. You are so—"

"Hey!" Bradley yelped. "Are you calling me stupid?"

Exeter leaned forward slightly. He was really getting into his tirade. "Well if the extremely small cranium fits, wear it." He bobbed up and down slightly as he laughed. With each bob I shifted to the side a bit more.

Until . . . finally . . . I had it.

With an angry grunt Exeter turned his attention back to me. I popped the top off the tube with my thumb. Hissing, he leaned close to my face for a moment then reared back. I twisted around onto my back. His teeth were closing in. I jammed the lipstick tube toward his mouth, frantically trying to ward him off. With a metallic snap he bit clear through the tube.

He froze in midbite, then tilted his head back. He wheezed. A wave of onion-and-sweat-sock breath washed over me. He made a sound like a cat with a hair ball, then gulped. It looked like he had swallowed part of the lipstick tube.

Then with a sort of fizzling noise, he grew limp.

And with a pop, he returned to pink-bunny form, nestled cutely on my stomach. It had been over in an instant. I had done it!

I had him right where I wanted him, and this time he wasn't going to get away.

I tugged on my shoes, all the while keeping a firm grip on Exeter's ears. Bradley stared at me. "It's a . . . bunny. How did you . . . ? It's a bunny."

"Yes," I said. "It's a pink, fuzzy bunny. Just like in my poem. Go ahead, give it your best shot."

"Killer bunny?" Bradley asked weakly.

"Tell you what. You can spend the rest of gym class trying to think of an insult. I have things to do." I walked out of the locker room and headed across the gym.

As I headed for the door, the coach called, "Hey! Where do you think you're going?"

Behind me I could hear Bradley telling someone, "It was a killer bunny." Someone was laughing at him, asking if he picked his nose out of hunger or just for sport. As I stepped out onto the sidewalk, I heard the coach saying, "Bradley, when you fainted, did you hit your head? Are you feeling all right?"

I started jogging toward home.

Chapter
Twenty-Three

There are a lot of things I expected when I walked in the door. My father, sitting on the couch with his tie undone, aiming my transport device at the TV, was not one of them. I watched in horror as he clicked it, vanished, then rematerialized on the couch looking befuddled. "Thing must need new batteries," he said.

The actual remote was sitting on the coffee table. I handed it to him. "Try this one," I said.

My father took it and began flipping channels. "Are you all right?" I asked.

"I came home to pick up a folder I'd forgotten. I stopped to watch the news for a minute and then I started feeling dizzy. Ended up taking a sick day. And the TV's been acting weird all day. Strangest thing. I'm not feeling quite . . ." His voice drifted off. "School over already?"

"They let us out early today," I said. I grabbed the transport device and headed up the stairs. My father hadn't noticed the fact that I was wearing gym clothes—or that I had a pink bunny under one arm. He was staring blankly at an infomercial for spray-on hair.

I set Exeter down on my bed and squatted on the floor, looking him right in his beady eyes. "You are toast," I said. He wiggled his nose and looked innocent. I wasn't fooled for a second.

I grabbed him by the ears and punched the transport button.

When I materialized in the squid-secretary's office, she stared at me for a long moment. Then she held up a tentacle. I stared. "I believe the expression is 'high five,'" she said.

"Right," I said. "High five." With my spare hand I slapped her tentacle. It was like slapping the skin on a bowl of pudding.

"The director is waiting," she said. I could have sworn there was just a hint of a smile on her face.

As I passed through the office, I saw that Mixto had fallen asleep, lying across three chairs and drooling blue goo onto one of the seat cushions. I considered waking him up, but he looked so peaceful that I left him alone.

The director stood up when I walked in with Exeter. He was holding what looked like a report in one hand. It was covered in red Xs.

"Well, then, of course, here we are," he said, taking Exeter by the ears. "Very good then. Yes, very nice. Well then." He pulled a cage from behind his desk, put Exeter into it, snapped it shut, and muttered into his intercom. He held the cage up in front of his face. "Young sir, you *will* finish your detention this time. You are doing an extra week for this stunt. I was really hoping you would be more responsible this time. First the giant slug in the teachers' rest room, then threatening to eat the Poetry Club unless they wrote an 'Ode to Exeter,' and now the business with the earthling. I am very disappointed in you. Very, very disappointed."

Axolotl popped into the room, took the cage with a little nod, then walked back out the door. As he passed me he gave me a little thumbs-up.

"Sir?" I asked. "Does that mean Exeter was a student here? I thought he was some sort of intergalactic criminal. Didn't you say he was very dangerous?"

"Yes, well he is quite dangerous to . . . ahem . . . unevolved species," the director said. "For an earthling, for example, he is quite a handful."

"But for you he's not a problem," I said.

"Well I suppose for more advanced life forms he is more annoying than anything else."

"If he was so easy to catch, why didn't you go after him yourself?"

The moment I said it I realized it was a mistake. The director leaped out of his chair. "Human boy!" he thundered. "How dare you show such disrespect. Puny little earthling!" His eyes whirled like little tornadoes.

Abruptly he sat back down, muttering to himself. "Twenty citations from the inspection board, explosions in the cafeteria, humans popping in and out like it's Take a Primitive Life Form to Work Day. Not even halfway through the school year." He leaned over and mumbled into his intercom before looking up at me. "All right then," he said briskly. "You'd better blow this Popsicle stand. Before we have any more difficulties."

I started out the door.

"Human!" he called after me. "I believe a member of your family unit was . . . ahem . . . playing with the transporter. Buzzed in here about a dozen times. Caused a great deal of disruption in the office, my secretary tells me. Ahem. Yes. We will be confiscating it shortly, but in the future, please make sure this doesn't happen again. We can only erase his memory of the interstellar jump so many times before we damage his brain."

The director's door swung shut behind me.

As I walked down the hallway, I pondered the past few days. I felt like a new person, but I wasn't sure why. My brother still thought I was an idiot. My parents wanted to ground me for eternity. Most of the people at school probably thought I was some kind of head case. I would no doubt face some sort of detention—although not the interplanetary kind—for skipping out of school in the middle of gym class. But I was proud of myself.

When I rounded the corner, the janitor was standing there, leaning on his broom. "There you are," he said. "I was waiting for you."

"Thanks for your help," I said. "The lipstick worked fine, although it caused a few complications with my . . . uh . . . social life."

"I knew you'd do fine," he said. "Don't worry

about the complications. Those things have a way of working themselves out. Are you ready to head back?"

"I suppose," I said. "But I was wondering. . . . It's not that I was expecting a medal or anything, but the director never even thanked me for getting Exeter back. He seemed kind of mad at me actually."

The janitor laughed. "That's how they are here. Don't take it personally. The director is under a lot of stress. He probably just didn't want to be reminded of how much he hates dealing with Buterians." He lowered his voice to a whisper. "When he was younger one of them turned him into a slime mold, and it took a week to change him back. Very embarrassing. People still joke about it—not to his face, of course." The janitor chuckled.

"Right," I said. "Well, I guess this is good-bye. I don't suppose I'll run into you again, so, uh, I hope things go well."

"I'm sure they will," the janitor said. "And remember—the director may not have said much, but we all know what you did. You made some new friends in the universe, and you never know when that'll come in handy."

Chapter
Twenty-Four

The next day at school Bradley never once looked me in the eye. At lunch he huddled over his tray, alone, poking at his lasagna and pudding.

I, on the other hand, ended up eating with Rob and a couple of his friends. One of them, a guy named Zen, gave Bradley a dirty look from across the cafeteria when we sat down. "That guy is so annoying," Zen said. "You know, he used to do this kung-fu thing every time the teacher said my name during roll call. I kept telling him 'Zen' had nothing to do with ninjas, but he'd just laugh and go 'Hi-yah!'" Zen karate-chopped the air. Then he turned to me. "What did you do to him, anyway?"

"Personality transplant?" Rob asked.

"Not exactly," I said. "I think he finally just realized there's more to life than eating fruit cocktail and beating people up."

"He's just staring at his food," Rob said.

"Maybe he's meditating," Zen said.

"Well, it couldn't hurt," I said. "He's had a rough week. Maybe he needs to cultivate some inner peace."

It wasn't exactly a perfect day, though.

After lunch I got called to the office to discuss the fact that I dismissed myself from school before the day actually ended. I got a week of detention. I tried to sound apologetic. Mostly, though, I was just relieved it was all over.

Detention wasn't that bad. Coach Targis sat in front of the classroom, his whistle still hanging around his neck, and watched all of us do not much of anything. I sat there and did my homework. When I was done with homework, I read a year-old *Sports Illustrated* that someone had jammed under one leg of my desk to keep it from wobbling. When I was done with that, I stared out the window. It went on like that for the rest of the afternoon, and for the next afternoon, and the next.

On my last day of detention, I sat at the desk and stared into space. I had run out of entertaining ways to spend my time. After about ten minutes the janitor walked into the room and had a whispered conversation with the coach. Coach pointed silently at me and motioned for me to come to the front of the room.

I walked up to his desk. Coach smiled at me.

"How has detention been?" Coach asked.

"All right, I guess," I said.

"Gotten your homework done?"

"Uh-huh."

"Want to spend any more time here?"

"No sir."

"Well you've been a model student in detention. What do you say"—his voice dropped to a whisper—"we commute the rest of your sentence to time served."

"Excuse me?"

"You're free to go, Sam," Coach said.

I walked back to my desk and grabbed my books. As I walked past Coach's desk, I paused. "Thanks," I said.

"Well my friend the janitor tells me you've been very helpful around the school lately. One good deed deserves another, and all that."

As I walked past him, the janitor winked at me. Sideways.